Meet Me On The Mountainside

A FAKE DATING FAKE ENGAGEMENT HOLIDAY ROMANCE

KATIE A PEREZ

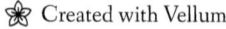 Created with Vellum

This is for those who would rather choke than read another holiday romance about gingerbread and hot chocolate.

Happy Holidays choke on a billionaire instead.

About The Book

This book has explicit sexual content and does contain :
    Talk of Cyberbullying/stalking

If this makes you uncomfortable, please do not continue reading.
    Your mental health matters.

Playlist

Spotify Playlist

Let's Fall In Love for the Night- FINNEAS
    Nothing- Bruno Major
    Easily- Bruno Major
    Make You Mine- PUBLIC
    Falling For You- Peachy!,mxmtoon
    Put Yor Records On- Ritt Momney
    this is how you fall on love- Jeremy Zucker, Chelsea Cutler
    Mean It- Luav,LANY
    Enchanted (Taylor's Version) - Taylor Swift

CHAPTER
One

Alyssa-December 23

"Chris, have I ever changed my mind about spending Christmas in the mountains?" You would think after eight years of not spending Christmas at our parents' place, he would have learned not to question my lack of RSVP. My family has lovingly called me "The Grinch," but it's not like I hate Christmas. I just don't understand why everything has to be so loud and bright. Why does everything have to be red and green with stripes and bows? There is so much beauty in nature this time of year; the snow falling on the tops of gigantic pine trees or the way flames flicker in the fireplace. I prefer to spend my holiday time off, surrounded by the natural beauty of Christmas and not the commercialized atrocity that the rest of my family has bought into.

"I send my love, but I will not be there. Even if I wanted to, I am already at the resort and the snow is falling pretty heavily. The roads probably won't be safe for much longer," I explain, knowing it is going to break my parents' hearts, again.

"I love you. I will see you in the new year." We finally hang up the phone as I pull into the valet line. I do not want to have to hike up the parking lot in the snow with my suitcase. I will happily pay for this luxury. A nice gentleman pulls my suitcase and bag from the truck as I hand over the keys. Walking through the entrance, I check the time; I still have a little time before I can check in, so I turn toward the bar. I stop abruptly as I nearly run into a man. I step back and take a better look at who is now in front of me. A tall, muscular man with his dark hair pushed back. I go to apologize, but no full words actually come out of my mouth. He just smiles at me as someone else gets his attention. He takes a few steps toward whoever he is looking at, and I take my suitcase and head straight for the hotel bar. Between breaking my mom's heart and embarrassing myself in front of one of the hottest guys I have ever seen, I need a drink. I find two empty seats next to the large wall of windows. The bar has an amazing view of the mountain and it is so relaxing to sit here and watch the skiers make their way down the mountain.

The waitress comes by and takes my drink order, and as she turns to leave, a familiar chest slides beside her. My cheeks flush red as the man I nearly ran into is smiling at the waitress, ordering something for himself.

"Is this seat taken?" He smiles down at me before he sits without waiting for the answer.

"I don't think it matters what the answer was." I smile. He lets out a soft laugh.

"I'm Logan. I think we were about to meet in the lobby."

He points his head over his shoulder in the direction of where our near miss occurred.

"Was that what was happening?" I raise my eyebrows at him. "It seemed more like you weren't looking where you were going and startled a young woman."

"Oh, I was looking. It's not often someone as beautiful as you walks through those doors." The waitress walks back and starts handing us our order, thankfully giving me a second to recover from his comment.

She hands me the hot toddy and I take a small sip, testing the temperature. The moment the warmth hits my tongue, I can feel my body begin to thaw. He takes a drink of what I am assuming is whiskey neat.

"So, you are watching those doors often? Are you a local?" I take another sip of my drink, waiting for his response.

"Not a local. But I do come up here pretty often. It's a great place to try and escape real life." That I can agree with. At night, the stars above the mountain range are something out of a fantasy; it's why I have chosen to spend Christmas and New Year here since I was twenty. I nod in agreement. We both take a sip of our drinks before looking back at each other and smile.

"Is your boyfriend meeting you up here for Christmas?" he asks.

I try to hold in my laugh. "Nope, no boyfriend. It's just me this year." Shit, I should not have said that. Watch this hot, charming guy be some kind of murderer. Just my luck.

"No family?" he questions, taking another sip. *Lie, Alyssa, lie.*

"Nope, they all went home."

"Where is home?"

"A small town called Northburrow, not many people

have heard of it." *Ok, you can stop giving this stranger all the information he needs to stalk you anytime now.*

"And small-town life just isn't for you?"

"It's not really that, they just like the stereotypical Christmas while I prefer the quiet and the snow." I look out the window and watch as the sun makes the snow on the treetops glimmer.

"That's one of the best reasons I have heard for coming out here during the holidays."

"Everyone else probably said this place feels like the North Pole or something pretentious about skiing, right?"

"Pretty much." We both laugh.

I take another sip of my drink and look around the bar, nearly choking on my drink when a familiar face turns my way.

Fuck!

CHAPTER
Two

Logan-December 23

I watch as the blood drains from this girl's face. I look around the bar for any insight as to what just happened. I follow her eyeline and see some guy walking our way. He has a shit-eating grin on his face while he practically is dragging a woman way out of his league behind him. Does she know him?

"Alyssa! I thought that was you. I didn't realize you still came here." Alyssa, a beautiful name for a beautiful girl, but why does he know her name?

"I have been coming here for Christmas for nearly a decade, Bryan. I am the reason you even know this place exists." She rolls her eyes. So they know each other well. I look him up and down closely. He is trying to come off as wealthy, but is definitely trying too hard. Every piece of clothing he is wearing has a different luxury brand logo. The girl behind him has a smile plastered to her face, even though I think she is as confused as I am.

"Oh right, I was wondering why I hadn't been here since we broke up. I remembered this place was perfect for a romantic getaway, so I brought Annabeth, my girlfriend." And there it is, he is an ex. He is laughing like they are old friends, but Alyssa is clearly uncomfortable. Why does he feel the need to rub his new girl in her face? What did Alyssa see in this guy, anyway?

"Oh, you are that Bryan," I interrupt. I stand to my feet to shake his hand. I have a good six inches on him, so watching him tilt his head up to maintain eye contact is actually quite comical.

He shakes my hand, asking, "And you are?"

"Logan Graves. I'm Alyssa's boyfriend." He lets go of my hand with a slight look of shock.

"Boyfriend? I didn't know you were dating anyone. You haven't posted anything about him on social media." He looks to Alyssa, trying to call her bluff.

"That's a weird way to say you have been stalking my social media, because I have had you blocked since you wouldn't stop DMing me when you were drunk." His face pales slightly. I look down at her, trying to hide my laugh.

"Yeah, my job is particular about our online presence so we have kept everything pretty quiet. It is what works best for us," I say after gaining some composure. Alyssa smiles up at me, a flirty glimmer in her eyes as I place my hand on her shoulder.

"What do you—" Bryan's question is cut off when a young girl looking through a black folder rushes up to us, slightly flustered.

"Mr. Graves, I would like to apologize about the wait, but

we are ready to finalize the plans for your proposal and elopement if you would like to come with—" She finally looks up from the folder she is holding to see Bryan and Annabeth staring at her, Bryan's jaw damn near touching the ground. He looks to Alyssa, prompting this young girl to do the same. She gasps and covers her face with the folder. I drop my head as Alyssa is frozen, looking up at me.

"Oh no, I am so, so sorry. Mr. Graves, I was told you were alone. I'm so sorry," the girl stutters as she looks like she is about to cry. I feel so bad for her, she didn't know what she was walking into and it would have been fine if Bryan wasn't here. But she just made this little lie a little harder to keep going. I look for her name tag.

"It's fine, Sophia." I take a breath and grab Alyssa's hand, pulling her to stand next to me. I position us near the glass window so the mountains are behind us. "Since the secret is out, I guess now is a good time as ever. Alyssa, I know this may seem fast, but I have loved every minute of getting to know you. You have made me smile more than anyone else ever has, even though you aren't afraid to call me on my bull-shit. You make me a better man. Knowing how much you loved these mountains, especially this time of year, I thought it would be the perfect place to create a new memory." I drop down to one knee. "Baby, will you do me the honor of marrying me and being my wife?"

The entire bar is silent as she looks down at me with both hands covering her mouth.

Please play along, please play along.

She drops her hands, revealing the most beautiful, genuine smile I have ever seen. She nods her head. "Yes, of course!"

I breathe a sigh of relief as the entire bar erupts in

applause. I wrap my arms around her and pick her up as I stand. Her arms fly around my neck as her legs wrap around my waist. Her eyes lock with mine for a brief moment before she is leaning her head in. Her lips press against mine and I tighten my grip around on her lower back, holding her against me. She begins to pull back, but I refuse to let her go and our lips find each other again, this time with a little more passion. The cheers of the crowd gain our attention again, pulling us both out of the moment. She closes her eyes and presses her forehead to mine for a brief moment before I slowly lower her to the ground. Once her feet are planted, I cup her face and kiss her as her hands hold my wrist. I know I have only known this girl for less than an hour, but the sparks in that kiss had to have meant something. If she is here for the holidays, I have a week to learn everything I can about this girl. I lower my hands, pulling her into my body, not wanting to lose any contact with her. I worry the moment we let go is the last time I'll be able to hold her.

"Babe, I know you had mentioned not wanting a big wedding and eloping, so I have it set up. That is, if that is still what you want, we can get married this week. Those plans were what Sophia was coming over to discuss. Since the secret is out, would you like to join us in that meeting?" I catch a look of pure disgust from Bryan, which makes me chuckle. I cannot wait to have her tell me what happened between the two of them.

"You set all of this up after that one conversation?" she asks, pulling off the "in love" look so well. If she has never thought about acting, she should definitely consider it.

"Of course, I try to take note of big things like that. They are things that are important to you and make you who you are." I kiss the top of her head.

"That would be amazing. Thank you." She reaches for her bag. "We just need to settle the tab."

"Already handled it." I smile down at her, earning me more raised eyebrows. "Sophia, if you would lead the way. It was a pleasure, Bryan. I hope you can excuse us, we have a wedding to plan." I stand between him and Alyssa, while she steps out of our little corner and back into the lobby. I grab her suitcase and follow behind her.

I place my hand on the small of her back and lean down, whispering in her ear, "I am so fucking sorry."

CHAPTER
Three

Alyssa -December 23

S ophia leads us to a conference room, she says another
planner will be in shortly. Poor girl, she seems new and
ruining a proposal is heartbreaking. Luckily, it was a fake
proposal, but she doesn't know that.

"So you were here for a proposal and elopement?" I ask as
the door shuts. Logan's shoulders drop a little before turning
around.

"If I answer your questions, do I get to ask some of my
own?"

"I guess that would be fair." I smile, my answer vague
enough that I can still say no.

"That's not an answer." He looks up at me.

"Damn, you caught that?" I laugh. "Sure, if you answer
my questions, you can ask me some of your own."

"And you will answer them?" he questions.

"Are you a lawyer?" I smile. "Yes, I'll answer your questions."

"Yeah, I had planned this trip for a while. Thought she was the one and she broke it off about a month ago."

"What happened?" I slowly walk closer to him, missing his touch.

"She had said we wanted different things. I like quiet nights in, she likes loud nights out. She felt like she either was going to have to grow to resent me for making her stay in or I was going to resent her for still going out, and neither was an option she was ok with."

"That makes sense. Doesn't make it easier, but at least it wasn't because someone fucked up." I place my hand on his shoulder. He looks at my hand and smiles.

"You were trying to talk to someone in the lobby to tell them the proposal and elopement were canceled when I ran into you," I say trying to figure out everything that happened in the last hour.

"Yeah, but the guy I needed to talk to was busy, so they said they would send someone to the bar to get me when he was ready, hence why Sophia came rushing over." We laugh. All of this would have been completely avoided if the planner was free when Logan wanted to speak to him. I wonder if he would have still noticed me and come to have a drink after he canceled such big plans.

The door begins to open and Logan immediately pulls me against him again. I can't help but giggle.

"Mr. Graves, I am so sorry about what just happened. I am glad to see you two so happy and it all worked out, but that was not professional. And definitely wasn't to the standard of service we like to provide here at The Briarwood." A bald man wearing a suit and glasses walks into the room. I just smile up at Logan, who seems to be genuinely happy.

"I completely understand, in all fairness, she arrived earlier than we were planning."

"Sorry, I was just so excited to be here and see the snow." I smile, playing into whatever story we are still telling.

"Which is what we like to hear about guests coming to The Briarwood. We would rather have you excited and too early than not want to be here." He laughs. "We still do want to make it up to you, so we have upgraded your room to the presidential suite and we have a table reservation for you at L'Entrecôte for New Year's Eve. We would love for you to join us and enjoy some of the finest dining on the mountain."

"I appreciate that, Henry. We will let you know closer to the reservation if we will be needing it." Logan's voice is more commanding when speaking to Henry. "I think we are going to head up to our room and celebrate after a hectic afternoon. Can we reschedule the wedding planning?"

"Of course, whenever you are ready, call down to the concierge and I will get right back to you and get those plans nailed down. I would like to remind you that you do have appointments already scheduled. If you need to move those, please let me know and we will do what we can." Henry nods to Logan then looks at me. "And it was a pleasure to meet you, Alyssa. Congratulations, you two make a beautiful couple."

He walks out the door and I turn to face Logan, who isn't loosening his grip on me.

"You're welcome for the penthouse."

"You should come stay in it with me." He smiles that charming smile that has butterflies flying around my stomach.

"I can't do that, I hardly know you."

"But you did say yes to marrying me," he teases.

"Yeah, because we were in a lie so deep in front of the guy we were lying to. It was the lesser of two evils."

"Well, I wouldn't have this suite without you, so you should enjoy it, too."

"I'm good. I will let you walk me to the front desk so I can check in."

"And then I get to ask you my questions." His smile widens. I roll my eyes.

"Yes, you can ask your questions."

He grabs my suitcase again and walks me back to the front desk. In line, he has his arms wrapped around my waist from behind and is resting his chin on my shoulder.

"You know you don't have to be touching me anymore?" I ask quietly.

"What if *Bryan* walks by? Need to sell the story."

"How does this story end?" I ask.

"With us getting married at the end of the week." I can't help but smile.

"Ok, but seriously, how do we untangle this web of lies?"

"We can just wait a day or so then tell the hotel that you have actually changed your mind, and want to wait until your friends and family are with you to get married. Then at the end of the week we just go our separate ways, and you keep the ex blocked, and he will never know." I think about that plan and weirdly it makes sense, and no one gets hurt, except maybe Logan's wallet. I'm pretty sure last minute cancellations are going to come with a hefty price tag.

We move forward in line as a young couple, holding a baby, moves to the counter. We stand patiently until I hear the young man behind the desk say something that catches my attention.

"I'm sorry, but there seems to have been a glitch in our system. That booking doesn't seem to have registered and that room is now booked to someone else."

"But we have confirmation and the funds were taken from our account."

"We will be happy to refund that to you and you should receive it in the next five to ten business days, since it does seem to be an error within our system."

"Can you just give us a different room?"

"Unfortunately, we are at capacity due to the holidays. There is no room to give you." The man behind the counter is doing his best, but knows he is leaving this family in a shitty situation. The snow is coming down way harder now and most of the skiers have come in from the mountain due to it. The roads will be tough to drive especially if you're not used to driving in the snow.

"Hey," I whisper to Logan.

He picks his head up. "Is it still ok if I stay with you?"

He looks at the couple ahead of us and smiles. "Of course." He lets go of me and ushers me to the desk.

"Hi. I'm sorry to interrupt."

"Ma'am, someone will be with you in a moment," the young man says, but I turn from him to the couple.

"Hi, I think I can help. My fiancé," I point back at Logan, who is looking at me in the most prideful way, "and I realized we both booked rooms, and I was coming up here to cancel one. Would you want to take it? It's reserved until January third."

The couple looks to each other sharing a telepathic conversation.

17

"Thank you. That would be amazing. When we get the refund back from the resort, we would be happy to pay you for it."

"No need." I place my hand on the mom's elbow. "It's already paid for. Consider it a Christmas present. When you get the refund, just put it towards the expenses this little one is racking up." I laugh. I turn toward the young man. "It's under Alyssa Scott." He smiles and starts clicking away.

"I have it pulled up."

"Perfect, go ahead and put it under their name, but leave my card details."

The young mom wipes away a tear and mouths *thank you* while her husband is giving the young man his information.

"Merry Christmas," I say before turning back to look at Logan.

"So, you're willing to share a room with a stranger so a family can have a room?" He smiles, beaming.

"You are my fiancé, and sleeping on your couch knowing they are safe in the resort is better than sleeping alone, worrying about them and their baby being stuck in a ditch somewhere."

"You're a special type of person."

"Dumb?" Spending two weeks in a hotel room with a man I met barely an hour ago is dumb.

"No, caring, compassionate. It's different." He smiles as he grabs my hand with his free hand and takes me to a back set of elevators. He presses his key to a scanner on the first elevator which then dings and the silver doors slide open.

"Penthouse means private elevator." He guides me, pulling my suitcase in behind him.

CHAPTER
Four

Alyssa -December 23

The elevator opens into a large foyer. I immediately walk over to the window and look out at the view. Through the snow, I can make out the outline of the mountain range. Tomorrow, when the sun is out, this is going to be a gorgeous view.

Logan scans his card on the keypad on the only other door here. It opens into a large living area. He holds the door as I walk in. The French doors to the primary bedroom are wide open, showing a luxurious, king-sized bed.

"Shouldn't I have carried you over the threshold?"

"That's after we get married, not after the proposal." I smile. I guess this fake marriage is going to be an inside joke he doesn't let die. It's kind of cute.

I grab my suitcase from him and pull it up next to the couch.

"Shouldn't your suitcase go in the bedroom? So you don't have to come out here to get into it all week?"

"No, the bed is yours. I'm going to sleep on the couch."

I take my jacket off and flop onto the couch, pretending to make myself comfy.

"No you're going to be in the bed," he says.

"Babe," I taunt, "you don't fit on the couch. You take the bed, I'll be fine here." I smile while pulling out my phone.

Suddenly, I'm being picked up off the couch and thrown over Logan's shoulder.

"What are you doing?" I playfully shout.

"Showing you that there is plenty of room for us both in the bed." He walks through the double doors and throws us both onto the bed.

"See? Plenty of room." He smiles. His hand is now resting on my hip as I lay on my side, facing him.

His eyes are locked on mine. There is something just drawing me in. He leans his head in toward me. The feeling of kissing him in the bar is the only thing I can think about, causing my core to tighten. I have never felt something so strong, especially not with someone I just met. I lean in and press my lips against his. He kisses me deeply. I part my lips and his tongue slips between them. His hand tightens on my hip before pulling my body against his. Slowly, he rolls over, placing me on top of him. My legs straddle his waist, pressing my core against his now extremely hard cock. It seems like the spark I felt is mutual.

He sits up, sliding us up the bed until he is sitting against the headboard, one hand placed on my lower back and the other sliding hair out of my face.

"Is this ok? I don't want you to feel like you have to do anything that you don't want."

"I want this," I say, rolling my hips against him. He tries to swallow a moan, so I repeat the motion.

His grip tightens. I sit tall and pull my sweater off, leaving me in my lace bralette. His hands slide off my hips and onto the bare skin of my back. I place my hands at the base of his neck, feeling his heart race. Our lips press against each other, heat rising through my body. I want to feel him against me, I want to feel the moment our bodies connect. I want to feel the electricity spark between us. He pulls away from the kiss and I feel the loss of his connection in my chest. He removes his hands from my body and my skin is suddenly cold where his touch once was.

"It's only fair." He smiles as he unbuttons his shirt and slides his arms out. He drops his shirt on the nightstand before placing his hands on my body again. My eyes rack down his chest, noticing the tattoo on his chest. Before I have a chance to put my hands on him, he flips us over. He lay on top of me with his hips between my legs. His body pressed against mine as he lowers himself to kiss me. My fingers dig into his back as his hips press against me. My core tightening as his cock rubs my clit through our clothes. Pressing his hips against me again, a gasp escapes my lips. He pulls back and smiles before sliding down the bed. He sits up on his knees before gripping the waistband of my pants. I lift my hips as he slides them down my legs, his fingertips leaving a trail down my body. After throwing my pants on the floor, he places his hands on the inside of my thighs and spreads them apart. Gentle kisses are placed on my inner thigh, climbing closer to my center.

"So perfect," he praises before sliding his tongue through the wetness between my legs. My core tightens, feeling his tongue press against my clit. He repeats the motion again and again, building the pressure, my back arching off the bed as he explores my body. His tongue begins to circle, slow at first, but gradually picking up the pace. I can't help but to start bucking against his face.

"I'm so close," I pant as he slides two fingers inside me. I immediately feel myself tighten around him. Stars begin to dance in my peripherals and I close my eyes as he pushes me over the edge. My body tightens as he continues to lick up my arousal. My body finally relaxes as he removes his fingers and sits up on his knees, a devilish smile on his face as he sees what a mess he has made me.

He lays back down on top of me, bringing his lips against mine, letting me taste myself on him.

"You're perfect," he whispers.

"I want you," I say, running my fingers across his back.

"Want me where?" he taunts.

"Logan," I whine. He knows what I want.

"Yes, Alyssa?" His smile widens, taking pleasure in this game.

"I want you inside me."

"That I can do." He kisses me deep as he unbuckles his pants.

Once naked, he lays down next to me, pulling my body on top of his. I straddle his waist, his hands gripped tight on my hips. He lifts me onto his cock, slowly entering me. His body tenses as he lets out a moan. I sink down onto him, feeling myself stretch around him. My body immediately craves friction. Slowly, my hips grind against him. I let out a breathy moan as my body reacts to him hitting just the right spot. I slow my pace as my hands fall to his chest to maintain balance. I find my rhythm and dig my nails into his chest, tension coiling up my body.

"Grab the headboard, baby," Logan instructs. I do as I am told. His hips begin to thrust as I continue to ride him, sending him deeper. I whine as I edge closer to climax.

Logan places his thumb against my clit, smiling up at me as my breath hitches with the new sensation.

"Just like that," he encourages, his eyes wandering down my body. His words push me over the edge as I cum around his cock. "Fucking beautiful." He continues to pump into me, sending aftershocks through my core. He swallows a groan as his body tenses as he spills himself inside me. The moment he catches his breath, he pulls me down, letting me collapse onto him. He kisses my forehead as I rest my head on his chest.

CHAPTER
Five

Alyssa-December 24

"No, please don't make me get up. Let's just order room service," I whine as Logan tries to pull me out of bed.

"How did it go from 'no, I'll sleep on the couch' to 'no, let me stay in Logan's bed'?" he teases.

"Not your bed, just the bed. I have a fifty percent claim to this upgrade, too," I say, rolling over into the bed.

"Fine, we can order room service, especially if it means you're going to stay in your underwear." I pull the covers up a little tighter.

"Don't be shy now. You were so hot last night." I roll my eyes. Last night was fun, but it wasn't part of the plan, not that there really was one. If anything, it just made things messier. Not only do I barely know this guy, but we are fake engaged and have now slept together.

"Yeah, well, we still need to discuss last night," I say, sitting up and holding the blanket against my chest.

"What about it?" he asks, sitting up and putting his underwear back on.

"Well, that wasn't really something we discussed when we didn't really discuss this fake engagement. I just want to make sure we are on the same page and have the same expectations."

"Ok." He stops and turns back toward me. "Let's set the ground rules."

"Ok," I agree.

"What are the rules, Alyssa?" He smiles. He stands and puts on a pair of jeans.

"I don't know." I fell back onto the bed. "I'm so confused."

"Ok so let's start small. Since your ex is still slithering around the hotel somewhere, do you want to keep up the fiancée bit while in public?" I don't know why, but I am enjoying the way Logan is referring to Bryan. He has no idea what even happened to us and is already on my side and despises the guy.

"Yeah, that would make sense," I agree. This place is huge, but I can almost guarantee we will run into him a few times this week.

"Ok, so are you comfortable with touching and kissing in public?"

"I guess." I shrug.

"Cool, are you comfortable with touching and kissing when not in public?"

"Like when it's just us two?" My cheeks flush with the thought of the way his body felt against mine.

"Yeah, like right now. If I wanted to lean over and kiss you, is that something you would be ok with?"

"I don't know," I say softly. I can already feel myself getting attached. I came to the mountains to relax and just take a breather from real life. I can't go home emotionally devastated over a one-sided holiday romance.

"Ok, well let's talk about that." He is looking at me with genuine interest. He wants to understand, not win.

"About what?"

"What is causing you to have conflicted emotions about it? If you are comfortable, you would have said yes, if you're not, you would have said no. So what's going on in that pretty head of yours?"

"Ugh." I adjust myself back to a seated position. "I don't know, it's just that I don't want to get emotionally attached if I'm not going to see you again after New Years." As much as my brain is telling me to slow down, I can't help but feel safe. He has never pushed too far or made me feel uncomfortable. He asked for my permission and has given me time to think.

"Ok, what if I am open to emotions getting involved? I already know mine are." He smiles like this was an obvious fact.

"You do?"

"Yeah. You keep showing me parts of you that I find extremely attractive. You are someone I want to pursue and get to know more, if you would let me."

"Yeah, I think I would like that." My chest warms with his admission. He wants me, and to get to know me. He wants to spend time with me outside of this room. He is willing to go at my pace. He is a walking green flag.

"Ok, so emotions are ok, so is touching in private ok, too?"

"Yeah," I say, smiling at the thought of getting to kiss him.

"Good." He climbs back into the bed and presses his lips against mine. After slowly pulling his lips away from mine, he climbs back to the edge of the bed. "So, we are keeping the fiancé bit going in public and we are kind of dating in private? Just going to see how this goes?" he clarifies, making sure we are 100% on the same page.

"Yeah that sounds good to me."

"Ok, so touching and kissing are good, now what about sex?"

My face immediately warms.

"Alyssa," he draws out my name.

"Logan?" I mimic.

"Is sex on the table?" he repeats.

"I'm not sure about the table, but the bed is a good option," I say, hiding my face in the blanket.

"Is that a yes?" He laughs, leaning in close to me.

"Yes?" He immediately jumps back on top of me. His lips press against my neck when there is a knock at the door.

"Sorry I should get that." I slide out from under him and grab his button-up shirt from last night.

"Uhm, I take back every argument I had this morning about going downstairs for breakfast. I 100% want to stay here and watch you walk around in just my shirt.

"Don't make me take it off," I taunt back, my cheeks warming as I realize what I had just said.

"No, please do." He smiles.

"Shh," I warn him as I reach to open the door.

I open the door to a silver cart being rolled into the room.

"Did you already order room service?" I shout into the bedroom.

"No, what is it?" He slides out of bed and walks over to join me at the door.

"From a Mr. Bryan Smith. He sent a note." The concierge hands me a card. I immediately am annoyed.

Congrats on your upcoming nuptials. Since I won't be able to attend the wedding, please consider this my gift for the bride and groom.

I roll my eyes as Logan lifts the cloche, revealing a platter of pastries, champagne, and a variety of juices.

Logan moves in front of me and wraps his arms around my waist. "Hey, let's enjoy the gift and get a little mimosa tipsy, and you can vent to me about all his bullshit. Deal?"

I look up to him trying to not smile, but with him, it's just so damn hard.

"Fine, deal."

CHAPTER
Six

Logan -December 24

We have now finished an entire bottle of champagne, and needed to call down for another bottle. We also ordered some food with more substance, since the pastries Bryan sent us aren't cutting it. I am learning that Alyssa is a bit of a light weight, and is a fun drunk. I don't think she is quite drunk, but she is way more relaxed.

"So tell me, why did you date that douchebag?"

"He wasn't always like that." She sighs. "We knew each other in high school, but always ran in different circles. He then went off to college and I stayed and went to the community college a couple towns over. When he came back home a couple years after graduating, he had seemed like he had grown up, that he had found a passion. He was smart and interesting. We started dating maybe a year after that. Right after we started dating, he decided he wanted to try his hand at growing a social media following." She stops to take a bite of her muffin.

"He found some success with that and got it in his head that absolutely everything he did had to be for content, including our relationship. Anything and everything we did had to be for content."

"And it felt like he was doing things for likes and follows and not you?"

"Well yeah, but my main issue was I didn't like my entire relationship being online. Like when you used the excuse that we were not public on social media because of your job, like that's my dream. I have even told my brother that I would only post major announcements on my social media for families, like marriages and pregnancies, job changes, things like that. No one needs to know I went on a date. No one cares. Plus, the more that stuff gets posted online, the more it's done to impress strangers or the people who see it, and less about what it means for the couple. It tends to be wow factor stuff, not the meaningful, little things."

I smile, watching her check more boxes off my list.

"And I had told him multiple times that I wasn't comfortable, but he didn't care, so I ended it. And when he no longer had dating content to make, his views tanked and he blamed me for it. His audience did get very protective over me which pissed him off, because stupidly he posted a 'we broke up... because she didn't want to be on social media anymore' video and of course, it made him look like an asshole. Which pissed him off even more."

"The reaction to seeing him yesterday wasn't that you still had feelings for him?"

"No, absolutely not. The fear of having a camera shoved in my face came rushing back. I was worried he would want to film me for a video 'look we're friends again, we even went on holiday together' to try and earn some brownie points back."

"He wouldn't actually think that would work, would he?"

"I don't know. I wouldn't put it past him."

"How long ago did it end?"

"Almost two years ago, we broke up on New Year's."

"Wow, and he is already bringing someone to your spot."

"Yup, I don't believe for a second that he forgot I came here every year, especially since it's where we broke up."

"So he brought that girl in hopes you were here to rub it in your face."

"Maybe? Probably. Too bad all it did was make me feel bad for her. Enough questions about me, you had way more than I got."

"Not true."

"Very true."

A knock on the door keeps me from arguing. I tell her to stay on the floor and I'll get it, especially since she is no longer decent. She's beautiful and I love getting to see her feel safe and free, but no one else gets to see her like this. I open the door just a crack.

"Your champagne and," he looks at the receipt, "two hamburgers and a pepperoni pizza."

"With ranch?" Alyssa shouts from the floor.

"With ranch?" I clarify with a smile on my face.

"Yes sir, with ranch."

"Thank you so much, I'll take it from here." I reach into my pocket and hand him a hundred dollar bill. I watch as he walks into the elevator and the doors close. I then pull the silver cart inside.

"Food is here."

She jumps up and stumbles a little, so I catch her. She lets out a little giggle.

"Sorry, I'm not that drunk, but I am anemic."

"If you say so, either way, let's get some food in you."

I place the food on the table and help her over to the table. The more she moves, the more I'm confident she is verging on drunk.

She immediately goes for the fries. The second she places a few in her mouth, her body melts and she begins to let out soft moans that sound oddly familiar. I smile, watching her. Having her stay with me could have gone bad really quickly. I am just grateful she feels comfortable enough with me to let her guard down some.

I had hoped eating would sober her up, but I think it just bought us time until the mimosas kicked in full force.

"I think bumping into you was the best thing that could have happened." Her words slur a little as she leans back against me.

"Yeah? Why is that?" I want to hear all her real thoughts, the thoughts she won't speak out loud sober.

"I probably wouldn't have stayed the full time if I knew Bryan was here and I was alone. It's hard solo traveling as a woman, anyway, but it's unsettling that an ex came up here knowing I would be here."

"Yeah, I can understand that."

"And dating you is just," she pauses, "icing on the cake."

"How so?"

"Well, you're everything he is not. You're tall he is, uhm, well, not as tall. You're successful, he only has the illusion of success. You are able to give me everything I want that he wouldn't or couldn't." This might be a good topic to stay on. I don't want to judge her based on drunk ramblings, but drunk conversations are sober secrets.

"What can I give you that he can't?"

"Orgasms for one."

I nearly spit out my drink. My poor fiancée, dating a douchebag for years who couldn't even get her off.

"Privacy, his attention, anything real," she continues. I wait for her to say something about money, but she never does.

"Well you're right, I can provide all of those things."

"Right now?" she asks with a flirty little smile.

"Depends, what do you want me to give you right now?"

"An orgasm," she says it like it should be obvious.

"Not right now." I brush hair out her face as a look of disappointment fills her face.

"But why?" she whines as she sinks back down into me.

"Baby, you're drunk. I want you to remember each and every time you cum on my cock," I whisper in her ear.

She pouts before settling in against my chest. It doesn't take long for her to fall asleep. I stand off the couch, pick her up, and carry her to bed. I take a minute to change into some pajamas then climb into bed next to her, turning on the TV. It may only be four in the afternoon, but she is out and there is no other place I want to be other than beside her. It only takes a few moments for her body to curl up next to mine. I'm going to miss having her in my bed when she goes home.

CHAPTER
Seven

Alyssa -December 25

"**G**ood morning, beautiful. How are you feeling today?" Logan whispers as I try to hide my face from the sunlight peeking in from the window.

"Mmmmmmmmmmmmm," I groan. I definitely drank too many mimosas yesterday. I'm surprised I'm even up this early. I guess when you get mimosa drunk and pass out by the early afternoon, waking up hungover at a normal time makes sense.

"Well Merry Christmas to you, too." He laughs. Even feeling like I was run over by a truck, his laugh still makes me smile.

"Merry Christmas, babe," I groan.

"Did you just unironically call me babe?"

"Fuck, it's too early for this shit." I roll over.

"Fine, we can revisit this 'shit' later, but you should probably call your brother and wish your family a Merry Christmas."

"Why are you being such a good fake fiancé?" I ask as I reach for my phone.

"Maybe I want to graduate from a fake fiancé to a real boyfriend one day."

"Hmmm, we will see." My screen flashes on and I am immediately bombarded with hundreds of notifications.

As I start sorting through the notifications to find some semblance of what is going on, my phone lights up with my brother's picture.

I slide the green bar over. "Merry Christmas," I groan.

"You're engaged?" he whispers in a shouting kind of tone from his end of the call.

"What are you talking about?" I shoot to a sitting position and I put him on speaker so I can continue to go through the notifications.

"Bryan shared a video of what looks like you getting engaged to an 'old money fuckboy'. What the fuck, Alyssa? Why didn't you tell me?" His voice shakes.

"*Old money fuckboy,*" Logan mouths, trying to stifle a laugh.

"It's a really long story, and a really short relationship." I smack Logan's arm.

"Ok well, what do I tell the family? They've all seen it."

"Fuckkkk."

"Ok let's just start from the beginning. Who is this fuckboy?"

"His name is Logan, I met him about thirty minutes before that video was taken."

"And you're already engaged? That is the stupidest shit you have ever done." Yup, that sounds more like Chris.

"Bryan showed up showing off his new girl, and Logan took it upon himself to introduce himself as my boyfriend to get him to leave me alone."

"What the fuck do you mean Bryan is there? And how did a boyfriend turn into a fiancée in one conversation?"

"I'm getting there. Logan was supposed to get engaged to his girlfriend on this trip, but they broke up and he came up to cancel all the plans."

"Ok?" He is still confused. Fuck, I lived it and am still confused.

"And one of the staff members came up and blurted out that they were ready to finalize the plans for the proposal. Since everyone was now under the impression we were dating, he just kind of ran with it and proposed."

"So it's fake?"

"Yes."

"And that kiss afterwards?"

"Fake."

"Did not look fake, the way he held your ass was definitely not fake."

"It was fake." I don't know who I am trying to convince more, him or me.

"Ok so where is he now?"

"In bed."

"Whose bed?" I can hear the disappointment in his tone as he is dreading to hear the answers to his questions.

"His?" I say, hoping I would still have plausible deniability.

"Don't say it's mine now, you tell him the truth," Login chimes in.

"Shut up!" I snarl at him.

"Alyssa Noelle Scott!" Chris yells.

41

"What?"

"Why am I on speaker?" I can hear the face palm happening on the other side of the phone.

"I'm trying to assess the damage that Bryan caused."

"Did he hear me call him—"

"Old money fuckboy?" they say in unison.

"Yes." Logan laughs.

"Well that's a great first impression of his future brother-in-law."

"Fake future brother in law," I clarify.

"Uh huh, fake." Logan laughs.

Logan can't wipe the smile off his face. I slap his shoulder again.

"Dude, you're in the video, too. Do you need to call your job?"

"Fuck."

"Yeah, it's not just my personal hell now." I scrunch my nose at him as he gets out of the bed.

"It will be fine." He kisses my head before grabbing his phone and walking into the other room.

"What the fuck, Alyssa? What should I tell Mom and Dad?"

"That I was going to tell everyone today, when I called. To them it needs to be real."

"Why?"

"They still talk to Bryan's family and he can't know we lied. We have also discussed real dating after the holiday, so if we break up later it will be fine, but if we do get engaged and married for real, I don't need it ever getting out that it started as fake. So you have to tell them that we met a couple weeks ago at my job. And he surprised me up here this week knowing I would be here."

"You really like him?"

"I do."

"You trust him?"

"If he wanted to hurt me, I would be dead by now."

"As long as you know what you're doing."

"Do I ever?"

"Not really." We both laugh.

"Ok, well, I will go handle crowd control for you. Enjoy your Christmas with Logan. Call me later, ok? I need to make sure you're not dead."

"I will. Tell everyone Merry Christmas and that I love them."

"I will."

Logan comes back into the room.

"Everything good?" he asks.

"For now. What did you tell work?" I try to switch subjects.

"The truth."

"Which was?"

"I have a fake fiancé that I'm hoping will be a real fiancé soon enough."

"They aren't going to be concerned that it has been like a month since your engagement ended?"

"It's not uncommon for the guys I work with to fall hard rather quickly." He laughs.

"Ok, well my brother is telling my family we are really engaged."

"You didn't tell the truth?"

"No, if I put the idea of it being fake in their heads it will always be fake to them, and if we do decide to graduate from fake fiancés to a real couple, they shouldn't know it was fake at all. And if we break up, weird, it's like we got engaged with each other after barely knowing each other." I start scrolling back through my phone and the amount of notifications for a post I can't see are overwhelming.

"Hey, let's put the phones away and enjoy our first Christmas together." He gently grabs my phone and places it in the nightstand drawer. "Your Christmas tradition is to run away to the mountains, my tradition is watching The Grinch movies. So come on, it's movie time."

"The Grinch? Really?"

"It seems fitting now that I am marrying a Grinch."

"I'm not the Grinch!"

"I know." He kisses my forehead and grabs my hand pulling me to the couch. "Come on."

He pulls me against his chest as I snuggle under the blanket. Maybe a few cliché traditions would be ok.

CHAPTER

Eight

Logan -December 25

The credits finally end as Alyssa lays sleeping against my chest. This is one of the first Christmases I have had in years where I wasn't surrounded by people. While I never disliked those celebrations, I think Alyssa may have a point. Spending the holidays away with those you are closest to and just taking in the magic of nature this time of year, is pretty magical.

My phone buzzes. I look down to see a text from the concierge.

> The package has been picked up and is being delivered to your room now.

> Thank you. Please instruct whoever is bringing it to knock softly, my fiancée is asleep on the couch.

Yes, sir.

I slowly try to slide out from under Alyssa. She slowly sinks into the pillow I was using as I get to my feet. I look down at the peaceful face of someone I met days ago, yet dread leaving when we go down the mountain. The engagement may be fake, but if she would give me the chance, I would do it for real in a heartbeat.

Love at first sight is such a cliché, but there has to be something to it for so many to believe in it. The way she looked up at me in the lobby, it wasn't even flirty, but felt like two magnets being pulled together. Then everything fell perfectly into place for me to be sitting next to her when her ex showed up, the wedding planner being busy so I was able to sit with her instead of being rushed back to the office. The new girl coming out and completely ruining a surprise proposal. Would she be sitting on this couch with me right now if none of that happened? She definitely wouldn't be if Hannah had not called things off. Which is for the better. My eyes look back to Alyssa and wonder when we are going to have the big discussions. Sooner or later, I will have to be fully transparent with her about my life and my job.

A small knock on the door gets my attention. She turns over in her sleep, but doesn't wake. I open the door gently as the young man hands me the bag and nods his head before leaving.

"Hey," I whisper. He quickly turns around, thinking something must be wrong. I pull an envelope off the entryway table. "Merry Christmas." His face relaxes and his lips turn up in a small smile. It's always the youngest and newest getting stuck working the holidays. Or they are the people who don't have kids or family traditions who volunteer to cover the shift of their coworkers, who do have little ones. I try to make sure if I utilize any of them working the holiday to tip them well to make up for it. He takes the envelope and whispers, "Merry Christmas," before calling the elevator. I close the door and turn to see a sleepy Alyssa watching me over the couch.

"Fuck, did I wake you?" I ask slowly, trying to hide the bag behind my back.

"Yeah, but it's ok. What did you hand him?" she asks, rubbing her eyes.

"I have Christmas Cards with $1000 tip inside."

"That's pretty generous." She smiles.

"I guess. I just want to make sure those who get stuck working the holiday get something out of it."

"So you are genuinely a nice person. That's good to know."

I laugh. "Did you think I wasn't?"

"No, I just didn't know if it was a facade for the week to impress me."

"No, I'm impressive even when not trying to win over my fiancé." She rolls her eyes before resting her arms atop the back of the couch.

"So are we going to pretend like I don't know there is a bag behind your back?"

I sigh. "You saw that?" She nods her head. "It was supposed to be a surprise."

"A surprise? For me?" She perks up a little bit.

"Yeah, I remembered how when we first met, you had said one of your favorite parts about Christmas was the way snow looked on the pine trees. And as a thank you for spending your holiday with me, I had this necklace delivered so you can take a little reminder of that feeling home." She looks up at me both intrigued and confused.

"You remember something I said off-handedly three minutes into knowing me? Then got me something because of it?"

"Yeah. Is that ok?"

"It's really sweet, but you don't have to give me anything."

"I know, but before meeting you, I was dreading spending the holiday up here knowing I was supposed to be getting engaged, and then I met you and every ounce of dread turned to excitement. I was excited to get to know you and excited to spend time with you. I dreaded having to say goodbye to you. The moment you brought up worrying about feelings getting involved, mine already were. So to thank you for being here with me, I want to give you this."

I pull the velvet box out of the bag and step closer to her while opening the lid. Inside sits a white gold necklace with a teardrop emerald pendant with a pure white pearl on the bail.

"A little bit of the snow sitting atop the pine trees." Her hands shoot to her face, covering her mouth.

"I take that as you like it." She nods her head slowly. "Can I put it on you?" She nods her head again. I walk behind her on the couch and gently wrap the chain around her neck and secure the clasp. She adjusts it to sit with the chain flush against her neck.

"It's beautiful, Logan. Thank you." She holds the pendant in her fingers for a moment before looking at me, her entire demeanor changing.

"What are you thinking?" I laugh.

"Well, I didn't get you anything."

"You don't have to." She stands and turns toward me.

"But I would like to say thank you." She grabs my hand and leads me back into the bedroom.

"Sit," she commands. I do as I'm told, sitting on the edge of the bed.

She unties the drawstring at my sweats, loosening up the waistband. Kneeling down between my legs, she pulls my dick free.

"Oh, so it's that kind of thank you." I laugh as I help lower my sweats a little further.

She wraps her hand around my shaft, gently placing the tip against her lips. She sucks gently as my dick hardens in her hand. Her hand twits around the base as she starts taking me in deeper. I lean back, letting her take full control. My dick touches the back of her throat and I can feel her swallow around me. My body tenses and my breath stutters.

She moans as she starts to pull me in and out of her mouth. Sliding me out of her mouth for a moment, she uses her hand to stroke the length my cock.

She looks up at me to gauge my reaction before making eye contact with me. Her piercing blue eyes stare at me as she slides me to the back of her throat again. She sucks harder, pulling another moan from me. She wraps her lips tightly around the tip and sucks harder while running her hand up and down my cock quickly.

"Alyssa," I warn, not knowing where she wants me to cum. She moans against my cock, sending vibrations through my body. She takes every last drop as I cum down her throat.

CHAPTER
Nine

Alyssa-December 26

The sun starts peeking over the mountains, flooding the bedroom with natural light. Logan tries to pull his arm from around me, but I refuse to let go.

"Babe, we have to get up."

"Noooo," I whine. I am on vacation. Why would I get up before noon? In turn, why does he think he can leave me before noon?

"If we are keeping up this engaged story a little longer, we have bridal appointments to get to."

This gets my attention, so I roll over and look at him. "What appointments?"

"Well, to start, this morning you are going to pick out a dress." His tone is so nonchalant, like he had just said we needed to get eggs from the grocery store.

"I have to pick out a wedding dress for a wedding that's

not happening?" What the fuck am I supposed to do with a white gown?

"It doesn't have to be a wedding dress, but I did rent out the boutique and already put a deposit down that would cover any dress in the store. So either you go pick out a dress or they just get to keep all the money."

"You're really losing a lot canceling this wedding, aren't you?" That has to suck. He must have planned and saved up for a while. Logan has money, that's obvious, but having so much of it wasted because the wedding was called off has to still hurt.

"Yeah, but it's not too big of a deal." Again, his tone is so carefree.

"How is losing tens of thousands of dollars not a big deal?"

"Hundreds of thousands, and luckily for me, it's not. Would I rather not have wasted the money? Absolutely. Is it going to ruin me financially? Not in the slightest. Plus, if I'm spending the money on you, it's not going to waste. So please get up so I don't waste this dress money."

Ok, so he is more than *can afford a wedding* rich, he is *I can throw away hundreds of thousands of dollars* rich. What the fuck? Who am I engaged, I pause and correct myself, *fake engaged* to? I slide out of bed. "I'm only doing this because I can't stand the thought of wasting that much money."

"Thank you." He smiles at me.

About an hour later after a shower and getting ready, he is rushing to get me to the lobby.

"Am I missing something? I thought we had like half an hour until the appointment, it's like a five minute ride into town."

"Can you please not ruin another surprise?" He smiles. I

54

shut up and reach for the necklace hanging around my throat. I still feel a little bad about ruining the surprise, but he seemed to enjoy the thank you quite a bit.

I grab my coat and slip my feet into my boots. "Ok, I'm ready."

He grabs my hand and pulls me into him. He wraps his arms around my lower back and looks down at me. "Have I told you how beautiful you are today?"

"Nope. If you would like, you are more than welcome to." I smile back up at him before he kisses me gently. How such a soft kiss can make my body feel so much, I don't understand. But I really like it. I need to remind myself that once we go home, it's going to be so different. It's going to be long distance. We are both going back to work. A holiday romance is fun and all, but the likelihood of this magical feeling lasting is very slim. No matter how hard my heart falls this week, I can't get attached, something I am failing at miserably.

Logan walks us out into the foyer and calls the elevator. We make our way down to the lobby, and the second the elevator door opens, I am handed a to-go cup filled with warm caramel apple cider. Logan is given a similar-looking cup, but I think his smells of coffee, and he is handed a thick blanket. I smile as I look toward him to see if this was the surprise. No wonder he wanted me to hurry up, the drinks would be cold.

"If you would come with me, your carriage awaits." I looked at the man who handed us our drinks. Did I hear him right?

I look back to Logan who has a huge smile on his face. "See? Surprises can be fun when someone just lets them happen as planned." He kisses my forehead before placing his hand on my lower back and leading me in the direction of the front entrance. Sitting out front is a beautiful horse-drawn carriage. I grab Logan's hand as I climb into the seat. He climbs in after me and places the blanket over our laps. I snuggle close into his side as the gentleman from the lobby climbs into the driver's spot and takes the reins. The beautiful white horse jolts into motion and takes us on our way.

I can't help but laugh as we were jostled around down the road. Logan's hand wraps tighter around me as we hit a particularly bumpy portion of road. I look up to see his eyes already on me. Before I have a chance to question why he was watching me, we pull up in front of the bridal boutique. The window displays are filled with lavish gowns with lace and rhinestones. A pit forms in my stomach. I am about to pick out a wedding gown, for a fake wedding.

Alyssa, it's not real. It's just a dress. The gentleman from the lobby gets down out of the carriage and offers me a hand as I climb down from the carriage, Logan just behind me. Once on the pavement, Logan offers me his arm and escorts me into the shop.

"Welcome," two women say in unison.

"Good morning." I force a smile.

"Ladies," Logan greets them. "This is my fiancée, Alyssa. She is to get whatever she wants today." He kisses the top of my head before letting my arm go. I immediately miss his touch. I frantically look at him as he begins to back away and head toward the door.

"Logan." I get his attention.

"Yes?"

"Can you stay?" He smiles as he walks toward me, grabbing my hands.

"I'm not supposed to see the dress until the wedding." He lifts my hands to his mouth and kisses them gently.

"I don't care. It's not like we're having a super traditional ceremony. Please stay." It's not like we're actually getting married, so it doesn't matter if he sees the dress. And I don't want to lose a few hours of time with him. We are only up on the mountain for a week longer.

"If you're sure."

"Sir, there are some seats over here if you would like to make yourself comfortable." The younger of the two women, guides Logan to the waiting area while the other walks over to me.

"Alyssa, I am Marjorie. I will be helping you today. Do you have any ideas of what you're looking for?"

"Not white," I blurt out, catching her a little off guard. "I mean, I want to be able to wear it again, like for special occasions."

"I'm sure Mr. Graves will be getting you many other fabulous gowns to wear for future events, but you're only getting married once."

"Babe, she is right, so get what you want even if you can't wear it again," Logan chimes in from the couch as the other lady is offering him every drink and snack she can find.

"I know, but I don't want the white to look dingy next to the pure white of the snow. So I might as well go intentionally not white. I also want to be able to wear it on anniversaries and remember the feeling of saying I do in this dress, to keep the magic in something tangible."

"Then it won't be white." He smiles. Marjorie smiles at me, trying to hide her disapproval.

"Do you have any styles in mind? Fabrics?" I should have thought of some of these things. Of course, they were going to ask.

"Uhm, I'm not really sure." I smile, trying to hide the

embarrassment. Most girls dream up the perfect wedding dress since they are little and are playing dress up. I never put that much thought into it. As an adult, my relationships never really progressed to a point where getting married was even an option.

"Ok, well, we will just have to try on a few to get a sense of what you're wanting. Let's start with color, not white. Are you leaning towards a pink or a beige? Or would you like to be vibrant?"

"Definitely not vibrant, I tend to stick to neutrals, so I guess more of a beige?"

"That's a start!" She smiles. "Do you like things more structured or flowy?"

"Uhm, Structured seems so formal." I look at Logan who is sitting back in the chair, watching this whole interaction with a look of adoration in his eyes. "What are you wearing?"

"Whatever you need me to."

Marjorie looks at me and raises her eyebrow. "He is definitely a keeper," she whispers.

"I think so, too," I whisper back before raising my voice for Logan to hear, "even though he is not helping." I hear his laugh as Marjorie starts to show me a few of the dresses hanging on the wall. She sits me on a barstool near the racks as she starts pulling dress after dress. After saying quick no's to several overly beaded and rhinestone gowns, she starts pulling some simpler options.

"I don't think I'll like the super formal ones. I just feel like for an elopement it's a little over the top and doesn't quite match the feeling."

"That's completely fair. What is the plan for your elopement?" Marjorie asks. I again have to look at Logan.

"I'm not sure. I didn't even know I was getting engaged

this weekend until a couple days ago." I laugh. Logan walks over to the stool I am sitting on.

"The plan is to go out to the overlook at sunrise. Say our vows as the sun starts to peak over the mountain range. So that way we are alone and in the calm before the day. We will get to say 'I do' surrounded by the beauty of a Briarwood mountain winter, snow on the tree tops and all," he says softly as I grasp at the pendant he gave me.

Somehow this random stranger from a few days ago has figured out the perfect elopement plan, one I would have never dreamed of being possible. When this doesn't work out, no man will ever live up to the standard Logan is setting. When Logan and I inevitably break up, I think that's it for me. I have felt what perfect is supposed to feel like, and it is all fake. How am I supposed to accept less after this?

"That sounds beautiful," Marjorie says, bringing my attention back to the problem at hand: picking out a wedding dress for a wedding to my fake fiancé. "I think I have a couple dresses that you will love." She quickly scurries to the back of the boutique while I am standing next to Logan. His hand finds mine and he interlocks his fingers with mine. I take a deep breath at his touch. While my heart is preparing for the end, it still finds peace in his touch.

"You doing ok?" he asks softly.

"Yeah." I try to say with a big smile.

"You don't have to lie to me," he whispers against my ear.

"I'm fine. It's just a little overwhelming."

"If you need to be done, we can be done."

"No, I'm good. I want to leave with a dress. I don't want to waste your money."

"Waste my money. Light it on fire, for all I care. I don't

want you to feel like you have to do something you don't want to."

"I want to, I promise. It's just..." I take a breath. "Bittersweet."

Marjorie comes rushing back in with an arm full of dresses. I see several layers of white exploding out from under her arm and immediately get hesitant with her choices.

"I have a few options, you don't have to love them, but I would like for you to try them on so we can pinpoint a more clear direction," she instructs as she starts hanging the dresses in a large changing room.

"You don't have to try on a single dress. If you want to go, we can go."

"But then what would I get married in?" I tease.

"We could get married in our pajamas for all I care." I stand on my tip toes and kiss him gently.

"I'm okay, I promise." I then turn away from him and head into the dressing room to see what monstrosities Marjorie has grabbed me.

CHAPTER
Ten

Logan-December 26

This appointment may have been a bad idea. She is not doing a great job of hiding that something is bothering her. I'm not sure if it's the pressure to buy a dress or if it's something I have done. We could be still in bed wrapped up in each other, instead we are somewhere she doesn't want to be. I finally hear the fitting room door open and Alyssa walks out in an ivory dress with lace from fingertips to the floor. It fits her beautifully. She has a smile on her face, but I can see the discomfort in her eyes.

"What do you think?" she asks, stepping up onto the pedestal in front of the mirrors.

"It's beautiful, but you don't like it." Her smile drops for a brief moment.

She sighs before responding, "I don't dislike it."

"You don't love it. If you don't love it, it's not the one. And you don't have to get something for the sake of buying something." She nods a little and turns back to Marjorie.

"He is right. It's beautiful, but I don't love it." Marjorie smiles back at her.

"It's a good start, let's talk about the things you like and we can keep looking." Her voice trails off as they re-enter the fitting room. I start to fidget as I wait for the next dress.

"If you would like to look around while you wait, you can. It could be a few minutes until they come back out," the young woman explains. I nod my head and stand to my feet. Maybe walking around will help settle some of the nerves that have filled my gut.

I walk along the wall of dresses, all the white fabric blending in with each other. The back wall has more variety in colors. If Alyssa gets a dress today, I can almost guarantee it will come from this rack. I start looking through a couple and not being able to picture what they would look like on a person, let alone on Alyssa. That is until I pull out a champagne dress. It's the right color and it seems fairly simple compared to all the beads and lace of the other dresses. It has simple, thin straps on the simple top and the skirt has layers of ruffles without being obnoxious. If I had to put money on it, Alyssa would love this dress.

I turn to find the young woman standing several feet back with a smile on her face.

"Would you like me to take that to the fitting room for her?" I smile and hand it over to her.

"Is that ok? It's not overstepping, is it?"

"It's absolutely ok. Having the fiancée at the appointment is my favorite, it tells us a lot about their relationship. It is also a lot of fun to see what dresses the men pick out, it shows us how they see their bride." She smiles at me warmly before walking to the back quickly.

I walk over to the couch, wondering what this pick says about me, and us. Does this give away that we barely know each other? Is it a good choice? My thoughts are interrupted when the fitting room door opens and Alyssa walks out in the dress I picked.

That's my future wife.

She has a smile on her face as she walks over to the pedestal. She looks at herself in the mirror, her smile reaching her eyes this time. She loves it.

"He did good, didn't he?" Marjorie smiles as she fluffs the back of the dress.

"Yeah, he did." Her eyes finally meet mine in our reflection. A sparkle flashes in her eyes before the joy disappears. Her smile is still plastered on her face, but her eyes tell a different story.

I stand and walk up beside her, still towering over her even though she is propped up.

"You're beautiful." She breaks eye contact and looks to the floor for a moment before looking back up to me.

"Thanks," she replies softly.

There is something she is not telling me, but now is not the time to press the issue.

"I'm worried about getting cold," she says trying to find any reason to not love the dress.

The young woman pulls several sweaters off hangers from another part of the store.

"That is common for brides, especially this time of year. So we have several white sweater options to choose from." Alyssa looks at a few and tries some on. She ends up picking a white one that crosses in the front and has parts she wraps around her body. It is shorter than the other sweaters, stopping right where the ruffles begin. Marjorie comes up behind her and pins some of her hair back before placing a veil in her hair.

She is stunning. I just sit back and watch as she takes in her appearance. She made me promise she didn't have to get a wedding dress, but now she stands there looking more like a bride than ever. The dress isn't white, and even if they took off the veil, all I can see is the woman I want walking down the aisle to me. She could be in my t-shirt and I would say the same thing. I am glad we had discussed being ok with emotions getting involved, because I would be fucked. In just a couple days I have fallen hard for this stranger. She may not become my wife this week, but I will do whatever it takes to have her marry me someday. I stand and begin walking towards her, catching her attention.

"Baby, is this the dress you will become my wife in?" I walk in front of her, wrapping my arms low around her back. Her arms wrap around my neck. She takes a deep breath as tears fill her eyes.

She nods her head while putting on a smile.

"I love you so much, Alyssa. I cannot wait to make you my wife." She nods as a lone tear streaks down her cheek.

Alyssa changes back into her clothes as the young woman explains that they will have the dress cleaned and delivered to us. Since no alterations are needed, we should have it tonight, if not in the morning. Alyssa smiles as she comes up to my side and stands on her tiptoes to kiss my cheek.

"I'm going to step outside," she says quietly before heading toward the door. I sign the paperwork and then quickly follow behind.

Once out the door, I see her standing off to the side of the shop with her head in her hands. I walk up slowly, not wanting to scare her. She looks up at me, her smile gone.

"Hey, what's wrong?"

"Just in a weird spot." She tries to smile, but it doesn't last.

"Talk to me about it."

"It's just bittersweet, you know?"

"What is?" I try to put my arms around her, but she pulls away.

"I just found the dress that makes me feel like a bride, one I want to get married in, but it's for a wedding that will never happen."

"What do you mean?" I look at her. Is she saying she doesn't have feelings for me? I just told her I loved her, did she not think I meant it?

"This is going to end. I know we both said we want to continue with it after we leave, but it's not going to work out."

"Why is that?" I plan on doing everything in my power to make it work.

"Up here it's like a fairytale, it's not real life. We don't have work or real life stressors. I don't even know where you live, you could be half way across the world for all I know."

"If distance is an issue, I'll move," I quickly interject.

"You can't do that," she argues.

"I can and I will if it will make you see how serious I am about all this."

"Serious about what? It's not—it's not real," she stutters out.

"It's very real. Every word I said in there was real. I'm not putting on a show or saying things for the sake of the story anymore, Alyssa. Whether it's this weekend, or next year, or ten years from now, I want to marry you."

"You meant it?"

"I meant everything. I love you, Alysaa. And I will wait however long it takes for you to love me, too."

She stares up at me, a tear sliding down her cheek. I move closer, wrapping one arm around her body, pulling her in closer to me as I wipe away the tear with my thumb.

"I love you, too, Logan."

"You don't have to say it just because I did. I will wait and spend every day trying to earn it."

"You don't have to because it's already real."

I pull her face in and press my lips against hers. Sparks fly between us as she wraps her hands around my waist. His fingers dig into my body as she tries to pull herself closer.

She pulls away and looks up, our eyes meeting.

"Let's do it. Let's just stick to the story."

"What?"

"Let's just get married this week."

"Are you sure? I will wait. We don't have to rush it. We can do it right."

"This feels right. Let's go down this mountain as husband and wife."

"Then we have another stop to make before we head to lunch."

"What's that?"

I smile. "We need to go get you a ring."

CHAPTER
Eleven

Alyssa-December 26

Logan and I walk hand in hand down the street to a jeweler. We step inside and shake off our boots before we are greeted by an older gentleman.

"Good morning, welcome to Harrison and Smith Jewelers. How can we help you today?"

"Good morning. We are eloping this week and I would like for my fiancé to pick out her dream ring." Logan smiles at me. Butterflies soar through my stomach as I hear him call me his fiancée and it is real. Up until this point it was all a lie, a story to keep Bryan away from me. Right now, he is proudly declaring me his. My cheeks warm as I hold his hand a little tighter.

"Congratulations!" He smiles at us, before looking back at Logan. "Do you have a price range in mind?"

"Nope, she can get whatever she wants."

"Well then, let's get started." He ushers us over to the

71

jewelry cases and he begins showing us several styles of rings. They are all beautiful, but they are huge and would catch on everything. I am guessing this man heard "no budget" and is showing us the most expensive rings in the store. Even if I wanted to spend all of Logan's money, these just aren't my style.

"I'm looking for something a little less traditional," I say sweetly. Fortunately for me, I have looked into rings a little more than I have dresses.

"How about we take a look around and see if anything catches your eye? Maybe something will spark an idea," Logan says as he walks us toward another case.

"You can get whatever you want, price is not an issue. I will spend the million dollars on that Asscher cut diamond. You smiled when you saw that one."

"A million dollars?" I whisper-shout. "I did like that one the best of the ones he showed us, but a million dollars?"

"Ok, we will not give the price for any ring if it's going to cloud your decision." Logan laughs over his shoulder, making sure the man helping us hears. I roll my eyes as I continue looking. I'm glad he's so nonchalant about spending a million dollars. I have never imagined being able to spend a million dollars on anything, let alone a single ring. I keep thinking I have an understanding of how much money Logan actually has and then he says something like that.

"Ok, so what was the difference in that one versus the other ones that had you liking it more?"

"I don't know, the cut? I like the square diamonds more than the round ones." I feel like everyone has a round cut and they are nice and all, but they aren't anything special.

"Ok so let's look for some." Logan leads me around the store, showing me several more options, and they all are beautiful, but none seem like me. I start feeling a little overwhelmed, so I stop and squeeze Logan's hand. He immediately stops looking and makes eye contact with me.

"There are too many options and I am overwhelmed, just like at the dress shop," I admit. This is all a lot. Going from never looking at a wedding dress to picking one is a lot, and now I'm in the same scenario as before.

"What would you like to do? We can leave, come back later or another time. We can get Ring Pops to exchange. I can pick a few out, maybe I'll get lucky and will pick out one that will make you cry, like the dress." He smiles while brushing my hair from my face.

"Let's try that. You pick out a ring that reminds you of me, and we can go from there." He nods, and before he turns away, I make him look me in the eye. "No million dollar ones. That makes me so uncomfortable." He smiles before kissing my forehead. Moments later, he is off asking about all the jewelry.

I fade into the background for a little and just watch as he deals with other people. His body language and actions practically command respect, but he is so polite and charming. He has been so kind to everyone we have met. The minute Bryan thought he had any influence, he became so cocky and conceited. He was rude to wait staff and anyone he deemed below him. Logan seems to have real influence and still remains so down to Earth and kind. If I had drawn up my perfect man on paper, it would be Logan, and somehow we just happened to be thrown into this whirlwind romance. I reach to my chest and twist my fingers around the necklace he gave me yesterday. He knew exactly what to get me after knowing me for three days. I have never received such a sentimental gift before. I pull out my phone and take a selfie, making sure the necklace is visible. I send it to my brother.

> Christmas present from my fiancé.

Still fiancé?

> Soon to be husband...

For real?

> For real

My phone immediately starts buzzing with an incoming call.

"Hi, Chris," I say quietly, turning away from the store.

"Are you serious?" he questions.

"Yeah, it kind of just happened."

"That shit doesn't just happen, Alyssa."

"Well, we were dress shopping and I realized that everything was so perfect, except for the fact it was fake."

"So you said fuck it let's get real married?"

"Yeah, kinda."

Logan walks up behind me, wrapping his arm around my waist. "I know you said I can't spend a million dollars, but I have a couple of options you have to at least look at."

"A million dollars on what, Alyssa?" Chris shouts in my ear. I can't help but laugh at the absurdity of what is going on.

"Hey, Chris, I'll call you back in a few. I need to go pick out my engagement ring."

"A million-dollar ring? He can afford a million-dollar ring?"

74

"I love you, I'll talk to you later."

I hung up the phone and looked at Logan. "Well, my brother might think I am a gold digger now." I laugh.

"Picking stuff out for you would be so much easier if you were," he jokes. "I would just need to get the most expensive thing. You like to make things difficult."

"But you do it and it shows me how much you actually care."

"So it's all a test?" he teases.

"No, but it does have its advantages." He leads me over to one of the cases we already looked in, but sitting on top of the velvet-lined tray are three beautiful rings. The one in the center takes my breath away.

I pick it up to get a better look and catch a glimpse of Logan out of the corner of my eye beaming with pride.

"You thought I was going to like this one didn't you?" I smile.

"Yup, that's the one that I looked at and immediately pictured you wearing it."

"That is a two-carat salt and pepper kite diamond. On either side of the main stone are three smaller diamonds. We also have a matching wedding band with a crown style setting to wrap around the kite diamond beautifully," the gentleman continues on to explain more details of the ring.

"Why this ring?" I ask Logan, wanting to know what he saw.

"You had said earlier you preferred the square diamond, so I only looked at diamonds with corners, and this one caught my eye. The diamond looked almost like snow and I—"

The moment the word came out of his mouth it was all I could see. I cut him off. "It's perfect. I want this one."

"Then it's yours. You will get the wedding band in a few days." Logan gently takes the ring from my hand and takes my left hand. Getting down on one knee, he slowly slides the ring onto my finger. The diamond sparkles in the light. It's the most beautiful ring I have ever seen and it belongs to me. I pull him to standing before throwing my arms around his neck.

"Thank you," I whisper.

"Anything for you."

CHAPTER
Twelve

Logan-December 26

Alyssa can't stop looking at her hand as I pay the bill for lunch. She barely ate because she kept getting distracted by the ring. I help her get into her coat before we head back to the hotel. We don't make it far from the restaurant when we run into a familiar face. Alyssa sees him first and immediately tenses and grips my arm tightly.

"I've got you," I tell her before I kiss the top of her head. Her grip loosens slightly, but she still has a decent hold on my arm.

"Hey, guys, how was Christmas?" Brian shouts as he jogs over to us.

"It was great. Where is Annabeth?" I ask, since she is conveniently missing.

"She went home early." He shrugs it off. "Have you guys had lunch yet? I am about to get a table at—"

"We just ate," Alyssa says sharply. "Sorry."

79

"Too bad." His eyes linger on Alyssa and now it's my grip tightening on her. "I see Santa brought someone quite a bit of jewelry for Christmas." Alyssa's hand immediately shoots to her new necklace.

"It was nice seeing you, Ryan, but we have to go. Wedding appointments, and all." His entire body tenses as I say the wrong name, but he tries to hide it and smile.

"It's Bryan."

"Right, sorry. Have a great rest of your trip." I lower my hand to Alyssa's back and lead her in front of me, making sure I stay between them. Something about this guy is off. I have always been protective of my friends, but none of that compares to how I will protect Alyssa.

"I'm sorry," Alyssa softly says after we get a few blocks away.

"Nothing to be sorry for," I try to reassure her.

"The more I see him the more anxious I get. He never scared me while we were dating, but when we broke up and he started going on long tirades about me online, that wasn't the guy I dated. It was like something had snapped. I thought maybe with having not seen him in so long it would have gotten better, but I'm scared it may have gotten worse."

"You don't have to apologize for his actions, and you don't have to apologize for finding safety and comfort in me." We walk the rest of the way hand in hand and make our way into the lobby. I press my key against the elevator scanner and wait for the elevator to make its way to the ground floor.

"I guess we do have to thank *Ryan*. If he hadn't shown up when he did, we wouldn't be here."

"We would have had a more traditional love story, but we would have gotten here eventually." I bring her hand to my lips and kiss her fingers gently.

"I love when you do that."

"Do what?"

"Kiss me." I smile as we enter the elevator. I watch as the silver doors close.

"Like this?" I bring my lips to her lips. I take her bottom lip between my teeth before pulling away.

"And like this?" I bring my lips to her neck, she lets out a soft moan. I reach to the control panel and pull the emergency stop. The elevator jerks to a halt.

"What—" she begins to ask but I pull her into me and kiss her harder. Her hands grip the back of my arms, keeping me close. I slide my hand up her sweater, brushing my hands up the skin of her back. She parts her lips, letting my tongue in to explore her mouth. My hands rake down her body, sliding into the waistband of her pants.

Blood rushes to my cock as she unbuckles my belt.

"Turn around," I whisper. She does exactly as she is told. I place my hand on her back and gently bend her forward. A soft moan escapes her lips as I lower her leggings.

Pulling my cock from my pants, I place it against her entrance. I slowly press in, my cock being swallowed by her. Her fingers clench into fists as my dick disappears inside her.

"You were made for me," I whisper as I slowly start to begin to thrust in and out of her. I wrap one arm around her body, pulling her into me. I want her to feel every inch of me. I want to see her face as I fuck my future wife.

I bring my free hand to the front of her body and slowly put pressure against her clit. Her breath stutters as I quicken my pace.

"I need my wife to cum all over my cock. Can you do that for me, baby?" I groan as heat pools in my back.

She whimpers out a, "Mmhmm." I thrust my cock deep

inside her, feeling her body tense with every stroke. She claws at the silver wall while she spasms around me.

"Good girl," I praise as my hips jerk with my own climax. Her body rests against my chest as the aftershocks dissipate.

I slowly pull out of her, enjoying how her body reacts to the friction. I put my dick away before sliding her leggings back up. I pull her in for one last kiss before pressing the emergency stop button back into position, causing the elevator to jerk back into motion.

CHAPTER
Thirteen

Alyssa -December 27

"Come back, your side of the bed's getting cold!" Logan shouts from the bedroom.

"Then stay on your side of the bed," I snap back from the kitchen. Being in a hotel, the cupboards are pretty bare.

"I'm worried it will be cold when you get back in," he playfully whines.

"Well then you keep it warm. I'm going to order some room service."

"You can do that in bed. It is so not fair for you to walk around in nothing but my t-shirt and then not let me hold you."

"You can in just a minute." I can't help but smile at the way he openly wants me. "Do you want anything?

"Just my future wife to come back to bed."

"I will, hold on." I quickly call down to the front desk and request a few things off the menu. I hang up the phone and head back into the bedroom, but stop in the doorway. Logan is sitting up against the headboard with a blanket laying across his lap. His abs and chest are on full display. My eyes wander over every inch of exposed skin. My eyes linger on his knight tattoo. I will have to ask him someday what it means, but for now, I'll just assume it's because he is my knight in shining armor. I am about to marry this man. In the span of a week we have gone from literal strangers to husband and wife. This kind of decision is completely out of character for me, but somehow it can't feel right anymore. Even Chris was on board after our conversation this afternoon. He interrogated Logan, but after telling him that I have never felt safer or happier, he came around and made me promise to bring him home soon so everyone could meet him.

He looks up from his phone and catches me staring, bringing a large smile to his face.

"Are you coming back now?"

"I don't know, it's kind of fun to hear you beg."

"Is that what I need to do? Because I will."

I laugh as he meets me at the foot of the bed. He sits with his feet on the floor and pulls me between his legs so we're chest to chest. He runs his hands under his shirt and settles them on my ass.

"Please come to bed, babe," he whispers into my neck. I am about to give in when there is a knock on the door.

"Food is here," I taunt as I pull from his grip and make my way back to the front door. He flops backwards onto the bed.

I open the door expecting to see the young man from the other day pushing a silver cart. My heart drops into my stomach when I see the face looking back at me.

Bryan.

"Hey, kitty."

"Don't call me that," I spit out at the sound of the pet name he used to call me, even though I have always despised it. "What are you doing here?"

"I wanted to talk, can I come in?"

"No, I'd rather you—" He stops the door as I try to close it.

"I just want to talk."

"That's great, but I don't. Now if you will please leave us alone." Seeing him this week has had me on edge, and something about the way he is acting right now is causing a pit in my stomach.

'I can't do that." He pushes his way into the penthouse. The closer he gets, the more I can smell the cheap liquor emanating from his pores.

"Are you drunk?" I ask, knowing the answer.

"Doesn't matter, we need to talk about this so-called fiancé." He steps inside the door.

"No, we don't. You have no business knowing anything about my relationship." I try to stand my ground.

He tries to brush hair out of my face before he stumbles, causing me to take a few steps backwards.

"We had some really good times, didn't we?"

"No, we didn't. And you need to leave," I say, my voice shaking. I look over his shoulder toward the bedroom.

"Don't be like that, kitty, I know I messed up, but I have changed." He steps closer to me and my heart races as my back hits the wall.

"No, you haven't. Don't you have a girlfriend you should be going home to?"

"Annabeth? No, we broke up." He scoffs. "She was a good place holder, but you, you and I are the real thing. I just kept superficial relationships around waiting for you to come back. We were such a great team." He tries brushing his hand against my cheek, but I push his hand away.

"Don't be like that. We need to work this out so we can go home and tell everyone we're back together," he said, his words slurring.

"Do not touch me," I grit through my teeth. He reaches his hand up to my face again, but suddenly, he is yanked out of my face.

"Do not touch my wife!" Logan shouts as he pulls Bryan back.

Bryan stumbles back to his feet, pissed.

"She is not your wife, she can still change her mind," he says, spitting his words at Logan.

"You're right, she can, that would be her choice. But it is also her choice when she says don't touch me or leave, which I heard both."

"Alyssa, just hear me out." Bryan turns back to me. "I can get you nice things, too. Come home with me, everyone will be so glad to hear we worked everything out."

"No. Bryan, this is over, we are over and you need to go."

"You heard her, let's go." Logan begins to guide Bryan out, but Bryan turns around and swings at Logan, his fist missing Logan and causing him to stumble.

Logan's eyes darken as he looks at Bryan. His muscles tense as Bryan tries to regain his balance. Logan draws his fist back before swinging at Bryan.

I hear the moment he makes contact with Bryan's jaw. I watch his body collapses to the floor holding his face. Logan shakes out his hand as he steps back toward me.

The elevator dings as several people rush into the penthouse.

Logan gently places his hands on my arms as he gauges if I am ok. The concern in his eyes is palpable.

"I'm ok," I assure him, even though my voice still shakes. Several men scatter around us, two picking Bryan up off the floor and leading him out. One man comes directly to Logan and I.

"Mr. Graves, I am John Kutz, head of security, and am so sorry about the intrusion. Is everyone alright?"

"Yes, we are ok. But he needs to go and never be allowed back."

"Of course, sir. If there is anything you two need, please let us know so we can get it squared away for you. We will all leave you alone for the rest of the evening," Mr. Kutz says before the men turn to leave.

"My pizza is still coming though, right?" I ask and Logan laughs. "I'm sure it will be up any minute." He kisses the top of my head as he pulls me closer. "I'm sorry I wasn't here quicker. I called security once I heard his voice, I didn't trust he had good intentions. "

"It's ok. I can take care of myself."

"I know that. I know you are more than capable of handling that on your own, but with me here, you shouldn't have to. We are a team." Hearing that my heart fully melts in my stomach. I have never wanted to be taken care of, I always handled things on my own. Hearing him acknowledge that he sees I am strong and capable, but still wants to be by my side and help me anyway, has tears forming in my eyes.

"Talk to me. What's going on, why do I see tears?" He presses his thumb across my cheek and wipes away the fallen tear.

"I'm ok," I whisper, knowing if I say much more, tears will fall.

"It's ok to not be ok. You are safe with me." His arms wrap around my body, squeezing me against his chest. At that moment my tears began to fall. I wrap my arms around him, pressing my face into his chest and cry.

When Bryan started gaining his internet status, it came with quite a few women wanting to throw themselves at him. I started receiving death threats from them, saying he would be better off without me. When I brought it up to Bryan, he just brushed it off and said it came with the territory. I had to handle it by myself, and when we broke up, it got worse. When I blocked him, his fans would feed him information. I had to stop posting on social media all together because he would just show up.

He hadn't done it in so long I thought he had finally moved on. I was finally able to have a sense of security in my life. Until he showed up on this mountain. I have dealt with this fear for two years alone, not wanting to bother Chris or my parents with mean comments on social media.

I am no longer able to push the stress that the constant fear caused down into the box and hide it in the back of the closet.

"You're safe with me, baby," he whispers in my ear. I pull my face away and wipe away some of my tears.

"Can we go back to bed?" I ask, and moments later he has picked me up and is carrying me to the bed.

CHAPTER
Fourteen

Logan -December 27

Alyssa lays resting on my chest after demolishing nearly a full pizza by herself. Today has been a lot. We made things real. She opened up about her feelings toward me and the fears that came with them, and then she said yes, a real yes, to marrying me. And that was all before her psycho ex showed up and forced his way into our room.

I don't know what made her say I love you and agree to marrying me, but I will not question her. I want her, and whether we get married tomorrow or fifty years from now, I know I want her.

There is a knock at the door and Alyssa startles awake, eyes immediately trained on the door.

"Hey, it's ok. I'll get it," I tell her as I stand and walk to the entrance. I slowly open the door, peeking out to see Mr. Kutz from earlier.

"Good evening, sorry to bother you. I just wanted to

come by and give you both an update on the situation from this afternoon." I open the door wider, letting him in. I look over my shoulder in the direction of where his gaze went. Alyssa is standing in the bedroom doorway, listening.

"The resort is pressing charges for trespassing and assault. Since we are the ones pressing charges, the police don't need statements from you unless that is something you are wanting to do. We would also like for you to know that he has been banned from the resort and will never be allowed to come back to The Briarwood."

I can hear a sigh of relief from behind me, and I cannot help but smile. Her favorite place is safe again.

"I am grateful to hear all of that."

"We also did get the majority of the altercation on the security camera, since the door was left open. That footage was handed over to The Briarwood mountain PD." His tone shifts. "I would also like to apologize, it was brought to our attention that the elevator cameras have been down all week. That was a failure on our part for your security." He tries to say it with a straight face, but that man can't hide the blush in his cheeks.

"Thank you for the update." I can't help but smile back at him. I look at Alyssa who is looking at the both of us confused.

I shake his hand before he leaves.

"What was that about the elevator cameras?" Alyssa asks shyly from the doorway. This girl is always the first to have some kind of snarky remark, but right now she is being so timid.

"Oh, that. The camera elevators were not working this week." I laugh.

"That's what I heard, but I don't understand why that's funny?"

"Well because they actually were working. All week. Including yesterday, when we got home." I can see the exact moment it clicks.

"No!"

"Yes." I try to hold in my laugh, but fail miserably. Her cheeks burn bright red as I pull her in close.

"No," she whines into me.

"I told them they needed to delete the camera footage from the last three days. I guess they figured out why."

"No." Her tone is so defeated even though she is still trying to deny it.

"It's gone, never to be seen, again." She smacks my chest before finally relaxing into my hold.

"Hey, let's get you to bed. Tomorrow is a big day, so I should tuck you in and then get to my room."

"What do you mean your room?" She pushes herself off my chest and stares daggers into my soul.

"We are getting married tomorrow, and it's bad luck to see the bride before the wedding day."

"A bride is also supposed to wear white and the couple should probably have known each other for longer than a week."

"Yes, but I also want to have that moment of seeing you for the first time walking down the aisle to me." She sighs, but agrees.

"So, let's get you to bed so tomorrow you can meet me on the mountainside and become my wife."

"On one condition."

"Anything."

"Will you stay on the phone with me until I fall asleep? I am still really anxious because of earlier."

"I'll do you one better, I'll stay until you are asleep and then I'll leave. Is that a good deal?"

"Yeah, I guess."

"Ok then, let's get you to bed."

CHAPTER
Fifteen

Alyssa-December 28

I sigh as I look in the mirror. I only brought my makeup basics, I didn't even bring a curling iron. I wasn't supposed to have any big events this week. I'm sure I can make myself presentable, but I'm supposed to be a bride today. I look at the clock and I have about an hour and a half until I am supposed to head downstairs.

> Good morning, babe. I didn't sleep well last night knowing you were alone, so forgive me if I look exhausted. I can't wait to make you my wife. I love you and will see you soon.
>
> Also, there will be a knock on the door soon. She is safe, I sent her.

. . .

I wait and as he said just a few minutes later, there is a soft knock on the door.

I walk over to it, still in Logan's t-shirt. When I open the door, there is a beautiful young lady with the most beautiful brunette curls I have ever seen.

"Good morning, I'm Emily. You must be Alyssa."

"Yeah, hi," I stutter, "Come on in." She walks in pulling a small black suitcase behind her.

"So I was told you are eloping this morning." Her tone was so bubbly for five in the morning.

"I am." Just thinking about it makes me smile. While we have talked about it, having someone else say it makes it feel so real.

"Well, then, let's get you ready. I will be doing your hair and makeup. Would you like to show me your dress and veil so we can decide how you want your hair done?"

After about fifteen minutes of discussion, we have both hair and makeup decided. I sit back and let her take control. Just shy of an hour later, she has me turn to look in the mirror. I'm stunned by what I see. I look like a bride.

She comes over and places my veil in my hair before leading me out into the bedroom.

"Let's get you dressed. We only have a few minutes until I am supposed to pass you off to security, who is going to escort you to the overlook."

I smile and nod as I stand and she helps me zip up the dress. I'm sure I would have been able to slip into the dress on my own, but having the extra set of hands was really nice. I hadn't given any thought into how I was going to get ready today, but Logan did. Emily knew my name, so she had to have been hired for me and not Logan's ex. He has truly thought of every way to make me more comfortable. This was last minute, but the memories will last a lifetime and he made sure every detail was perfect.

"Perfect, how does that feel?" Emily startles me, getting my attention again. She just tied the wrap portion of my sweater in the most perfect bow.

"Good."

"Not too tight?"

"No, it's great, thank you so much." I look over my dress still absolutely stunned. It's mine and this morning is really happening.

"Great. Let's get your shoes on and get you down stairs. I'm told Mr. Kutz will be downstairs with your bouquet."

My cheeks immediately redden as I drop my head back.

"Everything ok?"

"Yeah, just not super excited about the name you just said."

"Oh no, does he give you the creeps?" she asks, fixing my veil.

"No, it's just..." I pause, giving myself a moment to gather the courage to explain. "He had to erase security camera footage of my fiancé and I having sex in the elevator." Her lips turn up into a huge smile as she laughs.

"Girl, hold your head high, that's hot." I nervously laugh with her before sitting on the bed as she helps me with the straps on the heels.

"Let's get you downstairs, Mrs. Graves." I smile as we walk into the foyer and call the elevator.

CHAPTER
Sixteen

Logan -December 28

I stand at the end of the stone walkway, breathing in the cold mountain air. The space heaters I requested are keeping us just warm enough. I did not want Alyssa to be uncomfortable for one of the biggest moments of our lives and one of the first of our life together. I watch as the sun begins to peak over the mountain tops.

A few moments later, the officiant clears his throat, getting my attention. I turn to face the doors. I'm watching as the doors open to reveal Alyssa standing there in her dress, holding a bouquet of white roses. She walks toward me carefully on the stone pathway. Our eyes meet and there is a sparkle to them I haven't seen before with her. My chest tightens as I begin to realize, this is for real. She really said yes, she really loves me, and in just a few minutes, she will really be my wife. My cheeks begin to hurt due to the strain my smile is putting on them. As soon as she is within arm's reach, I offer my hand. Feeling the warmth of her touch soothes the anxiety in my soul. She is real.

The sun has begun to rise over the mountains, streaking the sky with a beautiful array of red tones.

"As the sun is beginning to rise over the Briarwood mountains, you are beginning a new phase not just of your relationship, but your life and your life together." I can hear the officiant speak, but my eyes are locked on Alyssa.

We say the traditional vows before exchanging our rings. I place the matching wedding band on her finger along with the engagement ring we had picked out. She slides a black tungsten ring onto my finger.

"I have the great honor to announce Mr. and Mrs. Grav—"

"Wait, did you even want to take my last name?" I interrupt the officiant, realizing that was one of the questions we needed to discuss that we haven't had a chance yet.

"Alyssa Noelle Graves has a pretty nice ring to it." She smiles. I never was one who got excited over having my partner have my last name. It has always been letters on paper to me, but hearing her proud to carry my family name warms my heart in a very unexpected way.

"Sorry, you can continue." I laugh, looking at the officiant for the first time this entire ceremony.

"I am honored to announce Mr. and Mrs. Graves. You may now kiss your bride." He smiles, closing the notebook he is holding. I immediately wrap one of my arms around her waist, pulling her body in tight against mine as the other hand cups her face. We press our lips together and the spark I felt the first time I kissed her is there again, but way stronger.

Time stands still as I hold my beautiful wife on the mountainside. Snow begins to fall, dusting us in the soft powder.

I pull my lips away from hers. "Mrs. Graves, would you like to accompany me inside?"

"Is there breakfast involved?"

"If that is what you would like, absolutely."

She smiles as she grabs my hand and we begin to walk back through the doors. The moment the doors open and we step inside the mirrored doors, we are greeted with a loud applause. Most of the staff and several guests line the windows on multiple floors, smiling and cheering as we walk into the resort. I look over to see Alyssa's face flushing bright red. I stop us in the middle of the walk way and pull her back in, kissing her just as hard. She drops my hand to place her on my neck as I throw my fist in the air like an 80's romcom. The cheers and applause get louder before I finally let her go. She smiles up at me and lets out an excited laugh. She waves to the onlookers as we continue on through the lobby. The crowd has started to flood in behind us. As we stand waiting for the elevator, she looks behind her and smiles.

"Hold on just a second." I watch in confusion as she steps back in front of the crowd holding her bouquet high. She turns and does the motion of tossing it. I smile as I watch women crowd behind her. She counts to three before tossing it over her head. A young woman catches it and smiles. The crowd begins to disperse as a young man walks over to the girl now holding the bouquet. He says something I can't hear, but as Alyssa walks back to me, I turn her around to see. The young man drops to his knee and pulls a small black box out of his pocket. Alyssa's hands shoot to cover her mouth. I just laugh, wrapping my hands around her and pulling her into me. I don't think there is a better sign that we are exactly where we are meant to be.

Also by Katie A. Perez

Light It Up

Burn It Down

Filtered

Call Him Daddy

Acknowledgments

This was such a fun story to tell. I have always loved the holiday season, so getting to write the first of three holiday novels in this world was so fun! Thank you for letting me be a part of your holiday season this year.

Bria, thank you for convincing me to switch books and not career paths. Thank you for running a lot of the behind-the-scenes so I can focus on writing. When I succeed it has a large part because of what you have done for me. So when I win, We win.

Nikki M, Thank you for listening to my voice notes and being such a cheerleader. You have kept me motivated and made this process so much more enjoyable,

To my readers, Thank you for supporting my little story. Whether you read my dark romance or are just here for the lighter stories, I appreciate each and every one of you.

Until next time, be nice to yourself, drink your water, and fall in love with every new story.

Veni.Vidi. Amavi.
We came. We saw. We loved.

About the Author

Katie Perez lives with her husband and two young children.

She is known for her dark and angsty romances, filled with strong women, powerful men, and the spice that carries them into their happily ever after.

When she is not setting unrealistic goals of how many books she thinks she can publish in a single year, she is probably drinking diet coke, eating salt and vinegar chips, and binge-watching reality TV.